Dead Girl

By

Andrew Gallagher

Table of Contents

Introduction

West Virginia Asylum 1981, a patient and a psychiatrist sit across from each other. The psychiatrist is a white man in his early 40s, thin, wearing a black business suit with a red tie, with blonde hair combed to the side. The psychiatrist is currently writing things down about his patient; the only sound to be heard in the pale white room is the jotting of his pen as he casually looks over at his patient.

The patient can be described as a young girl in her early 20s, thin, with smooth white skin, her hair is sunshine gold, long, with waves throughout, she's wearing a white T-shirt with the numbers 2-5-4-9 on the chest in small print, with West Virginia Asylum enlarge on the back in black with the same number underneath, matching white pants with laceless white shoes.

Unlike most patients, she's wearing makeup, black lipstick, and behind circles of black eyeshadow are deep cat-like green eyes, which are currently fixed to the floor; her hands are gripped around a porcelain doll of a young blonde girl in a white dress, nervously shaking.

And then a voice is heard...

Chapter 1: White Room

"Shelly Davis, is it? Do you want to tell me why you're here?" the psychiatrist says.

Shelly, now gripping the doll tightly, as she nervously struggles to get out the words. "I..."

"Go on..." the psychiatrist says.

"I did some bad things, Doc." Shelly says timidly.

"And what are some of those bad things?" the psychiatrist asked.

Shelly looks at the psychiatrist; her eyes are full of regret; she quickly looks away.

"I can't..." she says regretfully.

"Try." he says politely.

Shelly reluctantly sighs.

"Start from the beginning." he says.

"Okay..."

Chapter 2: Home

West Virginia 1978

Shelly lies on the grass of a beautiful summer day in front of her home. The sun shines off her golden hair. She wears black jeans with a matching T-shirt, denim jacket, and boots; black eyeshadow surrounds her eyes, matching her lips. The only sound that she can hear is the quiet but calming wind, followed by her relaxed sigh. It seems almost peaceful until she is met with the voice of her father.

Shelly's father, Alfred, is a tall, burly man with a horseshoe of brown hair, green eyes with a Stern, and a worn face; he dons dirty blue overalls with a flannel shirt underneath and muddy brown work boots. He seems annoyed at the sight of his daughter in the tall grass.

"Whatcha doin' girl?" he growled.

Shelly turns to her father, confused.

"Nothing, Daddy, I was just..."

Alfred scoffs and then proceeds to violently pick up Shelly by her hair, causing her to scream and squirm. He slaps her face, causing her to drop to the ground.

"Go make yourself useful! I got a shift tonight, and I need you to start digging holes," he says. Shelly looks up at her father, rage in her eyes, as she wipes the blood from her nose.

"Why should I?!" she says.

Alfred raises his voice in anger.

"What was that?!" he barked.

Shelly then starts to run away.

"WHERE YOU RUNNING TO, Girl?! You ain't got no place to run to! Just wait until you get home!"

Shelly hears these words in the distance as she makes her way to the local graveyard, not to help with her father's shift as a grave digger, but it is merely a sanctuary as the sun sets.

Chapter 3: The Graveyard

Shelly finds herself at the gates of the graveyard; they are unlocked, so she pushes her way through and lets herself in. She then takes a stroll, looking at each headstone, admiring them, but at the same time looking for something; she finds an open grave with a casket inside. Fascinated, she walks towards it, puts her hand on the casket, opens it, and finds the corpse of a young boy roughly her age inside.

She smiles; the corpse seems to be untouched, fresh.

She caresses his cheeks and says, "Hello there, pretty boy, a shame that somebody left you out here like this; you must be lonely."

She takes her hand off the corpse and closes the casket.

"Can't leave you like this." she says sympathetically.

She then finds a shovel nearby and begins to fill the rest of the hole until nightfall, when the moon shines, giving the sky a bluish glow.

She sighs, puts down the shovel, and leans against a tall headstone with her arms crossed.

She says to the corpse, "My Daddy's right, you know... ain't got no place to go..."

Then to herself, "No place at all..."

She starts to head back home reluctantly.

Chapter 4: Mama

Shelly creeps quietly into the back of the house through a screen door leading to the den. The inside is rural yet cozy as if straight out of a 1960s magazine; the den has a warm brown color scheme, with a black and white TV, a coffee table centered in the room, behind the table, against a beige wall, is a brown leather couch with two tall lamps on each side, with a matching recliner slightly off to the left. Finally, an end table houses a small record player.

Shelly hears her mother's voice calling her; she reluctantly makes her way into the kitchen. The kitchen is a pristine white, much like an asylum, with wooden cabinets, and matching tile floor, a black island in the center of the room, and steps off to the right corner, leading to the basement furnace. In the kitchen, Shelly's mother, Alice, is chopping vegetables on the island.

Shelly's mother can be best described as a middle-aged woman, thin with white skin with dirty blond hair that looks like a mess of brown barb wire, that has long lost its golden shine, only having strands of yellow hair throughout the tangled mess, she wears a blue Floral pattern dress, with sharp black heels. Her face is worn down with crow's feet around her icy blue eyes; she speaks with an uneasy calmness in her voice.

"Shelly?"

Shelly's voice trembles, "Yes, Ma'am?"

"I heard you had to fight with your father today," Alice says, keeping the calmness in her voice.

The chopping of the knife seems to get louder and louder in Shelly's mind as all other sounds drain out.

"Yes, Ma'am..." Shelly reluctantly replies.

"What was that?" Alice asks.

"Yes, Ma'am," Shelly quivers.

"I see..." Alice says causally.

Alice turns to face Shelly; her eyes seem cold and lifeless.

"Strip." she says coldly.

Shelly tries to explain, "Mama, I…"

"NOW, SHELLY!" Alice demands.

As Shelly begins to strip down to her bra and underwear, she begs and pleads, "Please, mama, I didn't mean to, don't make me do this; I don't want to do this."

As she begins to cry, Alice points to the floor.

"Down." she says.

Shelly begs again, "Please, mama, I'm sorry..." "Down,

Shelly!" Alice says in a stern voice.

Shelly's sobbing louder as she gets on all fours.

And with a sadistic smile on her face, Alice turns to her husband.

"Al?" she says gleefully.

Shelly begins to plead once more, this time louder, as her father takes off his belt.

"PLEASE, MAMA, I'M SORRY!"

Alfred begins whipping Shelly's Back with his belt.

Shelly screams and cries as she is whipped repeatedly, forming red welts on her back and eventually, over time, being slashed open, leaving flashes of red blood, but then, the psychiatrist's voice can be heard, calling Shelly's name, pulling her out of the horrible memory.

Chapter 5:
White Walls, Warm Heart

Shelly finds herself back at the asylum, her hands shaking frantically around the doll, and her eyes fill with tears as the memory has caused her to break into a manic crying fit. The psychiatrist takes her hand gently, stopping her crying instantaneously and bringing her back to reality.

"Are you ok, Shelly?"

The psychiatrist takes a handkerchief from his breast pocket.

"May I?" he asks politely.

Shelly leans forward as the psychiatrist wipes her tears away and smiles.

"There we are."

"That's enough for today."

She sighs in relief.

A pair of orderlies come to greet Shelly, both holding a straight jacket, in a very polite manner with the back facing out unstrapped, as if handing Shelly her coat.

"Ready, Miss Davis?" one of the orderlies says.

Shelly gives them her doll, slips into the straight jacket arms first, then one of the orderlies does the straps in the back and turns her around. Shelly then Smiles at the psychiatrist again.

"Ready." she says.

Chapter 6: Thanks Doc

The next day, Shelly is brought to the psychiatrist to join him again in the White room, accompanied by a pair of orderlies, she sits down, and they remove her straight jacket, then they exit the room. However, Shelly seems to make more eye contact with the psychiatrist, even sneaking in a smile before shyly putting her head down when he notices before piping up with... "Um... Doc, I wanted to... thank you for..." "Yesterday?" he replies.

Shelly continues, "Yeah... no one's ever." "Comforted

you?" he answers.

"Yeah... not for a while." she replies.

"Not for a while?" he says.

Then he asks, "This was someone you knew?"

"Yes." Shelly replies.

"And they made you feel safe?" he asks.

"More than that, Doc, he..." Shelly

pauses.

Then she tries to speak, "I…"

The psychiatrist then asks, "Continue where we left off, and if you can, tell me a little bit about him?" he says.

Shelly, now looking at the floor, smiles again.

"Okay, I'll try..." she says, trying to gain the courage.

Chapter 7: Dolly

The whipping then stops leaving Shelly with gashes in her back. Quietly sobbing, she picks up her clothes and heads off to her room. Inside, Shelly's room is mostly empty, with a small bed on the floor and a dusty mattress. The room is small, with dark blue walls that seemed to be barely painted, only one window with a white silk curtain, and finally, at the far end of the room, houses a shelf with a doll that seemed to be homemade. Made of stitching fabric and other sewing materials such as buttons for eyes, with a mouth sewed into it.

Shelly goes over to the shelf, grabs the doll, brings it to the bed, and gently caresses it. She then says to the doll, "I don't know what to do anymore."

"We've been living like this for a long time now, and I'm still scared that it will never go away."

She holds up the doll in front of her.

"What should I do?"

She listens to the doll.

"No."

She looks around.

"How?"

She then holds the doll close to her chest and thinks.

"Maybe, maybe."

Chapter 8: Him

The next day, Shelly starts packing her things for school, then heads off to the bus. As she walks to her seat on the bus, she is greeted with stares and scowls, some giggled at her expense. While others choose to look away or take her as an inconvenience.

It seems like the longest walk in the world for Shelly; she quietly keeps her head down, books in hand, staring at the floor and occasionally looking for someone, who seems to be all the way in the back of the bus, but then she spots him.

The boy is raising his arm with a cheerful smile.

The boy has baby blue eyes, white skin with long dirty blonde hair which hides his face slightly, blue jeans, and a dark brown bomber jacket with a white T-shirt underneath.

"Shelly!" the boy calls out.

Shelly's face lights up with joy as she wears a very rosy smile.

She then picks up the pace, and her slow walk almost becomes a playful skip as she heads in this boy's direction.

However, this moment of joy is broken by her knocking ever so slightly into someone's shoulder, and then a voice pipes up, with a "Watch where you're going, Barbie!" a voice that Shelly was too familiar with.

The voice belongs to a girl sitting across from Shelly; she is dressed in a white button-down with short sleeves, a black ascot around her neck, a black buttoned-down skirt topped off with a belt with a gold hoop in the center, and with white stockings.

The girl has dirty brown hair that is blown out, smooth white skin, deep blue eyes, and ruby red lips. Behind the girl was her two twin sisters, Dee Dee and Dot, wearing the same clothes minus the ascot: they all giggled.

The boy then pipes up with...

"Leave her alone, Deidre!"

Deidre says, "Aww, what's the matter, Tommy? Did I hurt your girlfriend's feelings?"

Tommy pats the seat next to him.

Tommy says, "Sit right here, Shelly, just ignore them."

Shelly slides next to Tommy and looks at the floor.

Deidre says to Shelly, "Hey, freak! Blondie, hey, I'm talking to you!"

Shelly looks over at Deidre.

Deidre asks, "Doesn't your daddy bury corpses for a living?"

Dee Dee says, "Oh yeah."

Dot says, "That's right!"

Deidre says, "I bet he fucks them too. Is that where he found you? In a hole somewhere? I mean, that explains why your face is so fucked up! It's probably rotting from the inside."

Deirdre laughs and says, "Daddy's little dead girl."

The sisters chant daddy's little dead girl twice and laugh.

Tommy then stands up, facing the girls.

"I said knock it off!" he shouts.

All the sisters simultaneously sarcastically oohs.

Deidre says, "Looks like Prince Charming's got a set down there."

Then she asks, "Whaca ya gonna do, huh?"

Deidre pulls out a switchblade from her stocking and flips out the blade.

The other two sisters chant whacha ya gonna do, as Deidre waves the blade back and forth slowly.

The bus doors open; they arrive at school.

Deidre notices the kids exiting the bus, she looks back at Tommy with a wicked smile.

Deidre cheerfully says, "Whoops, saved by the Bell."

Her sisters begin to exit the bus; Deidre is bouncing her blade on her shoulder still in Tommy's direction while watching her sisters leave; before following, she looks back at Shelly and Tommy with the same wicked smile as she leaves with these words...

First cheerfully, "We'll see you two later."

"And remember..."

She points the blade at Tommy.

Then sternly, "Don't try anything cute!"

Chapter 9: Hallway Part 1

Later Shelly and Tommy are on their way to the lunchroom when they spot the sisters in the distance across from them in the hallway.

Shelly locks on to Deidre; her eyes are trying to burn a hole through the back of her head.

Deidre turns and glances at Shelly with a sadistic smile, then turns away and continues to chat with her sisters.

Tommy puts his hand on Shelly's shoulder and says...

"Don't worry about them, come on, let's go."

Shelly and Tommy head off to the lunchroom.

Chapter 10: Lunchtime

Shelly and Tommy sit across from each other at the lunch table, with trays housing a sandwich and an apple with a small milk carton.

Shelly's still thinking about what Deidre said and the laughter of the two sisters as she solemnly looks down at her tray.

"Hey" Tommy says.

Shelly looks up at Tommy.

He has two straws on the side of his mouth that look like walrus tusks.

He begins to growl and make other ridiculous noises.

Shelly begins to giggle before bursting into full-blown laughter.

Tommy then puts straws on the side of his lips and pretends to stroke a large mustache, Shelly smiles.

He puts the straws down and smirks back.

Then he says, "You know, you're really pretty when you smile."

Shelly then takes a big bite of her sandwich, holds it in her mouth, and smiles, exposing the food.

Tommy laughs and says, "That's nasty!"

He laughs again.

Shelly swallows her food and says in a coy manner, "Still think I'm pretty?"

"Ah, she speaks!" he says jokingly.

"Of mouth and mind," she says enthusiastically.

"Uh oh, look out now." he says, still joking.

They both laugh.

Tommy asks, "Hey did you see last week's Monster Mash?"

Shelly replies, "No, I missed it. Daddy came home early."

Tommy says, "Really? That's too bad."

Shelly replies, "Yeah, it ain't always easy sneaking around to watch your favorite shows."

Tommy says, "You could have come to my place."

Shelly replies, "Daddy doesn't like me sneaking out."

Tommy, now concerned, says, "Do they still?"

Shelly replies, "Yes... you've seen the scars..."

Tommy becomes frustrated and says...

"It is not right! I wish I could just… do something!"

Shelly reaches out, placing her hand on Tommy's own.

She says softly, "One day we'll figure this out, don't worry, I'm a big girl, I'll be fine."

"Well, if you need anything…" he says.

"I know." she says.

"And Tommy..."

She gently rubs the top of his hand and says, "Thank you."

"For what?" he asks.

"For sticking up for me on the bus this morning," she says.

"Oh, that, it was nothing." he says casually.

Then he asks, "You have gym class next?"

Shelly solemnly looks down at the table and says, "Yeah." Tommy, again concerned, says, "With Deidre and her sisters?"

"Yeah..." she says.

Tommy then asks, "If you want me to come with you."

Shelly replies, "You can't."

Shelly looks at Tommy and says.

"What are you going to do? Follow me into the girl's locker room? The last thing I want for you, Tom Tom, is for the school to think you're some type of pervert and suspend you."

Tommy then replies, "Then take this."

Tommy reaches into his jacket pocket, pulls out a switchblade, and hands it to Shelly.

"I couldn't use this on the bus; I didn't want anybody getting suspicious, how Deidre got away with it; I guess popularity has its perks but, keep it close by; I'm sure they'll try something."

Shelly puts it in her jacket pocket, then she hugs Tommy tightly.

"Thank you." she says.

Tommy blushes.

Shelly looks at Tommy and smiles.

"Um... Tommy?"

Tommy, now embarrassed, "Oh, um..."

"You falling for me, Tom Tom?" she says, teasing him.

Tommy nervously laughs, then clears his throat and says, "Just… just be careful."

Chapter 11: Something More?

In the present day, we find the psychiatrist jotting down the details of Shelly's memory.

The psychiatrist says, "I see. This Tommy seems like a good friend; he protected you, didn't he?"

"Yes." Shelly says.

The psychiatrist then asks, "And how long have you known each other? Since childhood, am I correct?"

Shelly replies, "That's right, I met him when I was 8 years old."

The psychiatrist says, "But it sounds like you two were something more."

Shelly smiles, blushes slightly, then turns away, clutching her doll tightly.

The psychiatrist chuckles and smiles in kind.

The psychiatrist says, "I'd love to hear more tomorrow."

"Okay."

The orderlies bring her a straight jacket just as before; she hands one of them her doll, and they take her away quietly as the psychiatrist calls out...

"See you tomorrow, Miss Davis."

Shelly turns her head slightly to face him with a smile.

Shelly replies, " Thanks for listening again, Doc."

The psychiatrist looks up and smiles back.

The next day, the two meet again.

"Hello, Shelly. How are we today?"

Shelly smiles and replies, "We're fine, Doc."

He smiles back; he then asks, "That's good. Shall we continue from where we left off?"

"Sure."

Chapter 12: Fight!

At the end of gym class, the gym teacher Ms. Flounder is having a smoke break outside the gymnasium; she is best described as a tall masculine woman with a worn-out face, greasy Brown hair tied in a bun, dressed in black shorts, long tube socks, black sneakers, and an orange T-shirt, with a whistle around her neck.

Shelly is dressing in the girl's locker room; she is crouching by her locker, still in her bra and panties, making sure to keep Tommy's switchblade close by; she periodically glances at Deidre and her sisters from behind until Shelly is spotted by Deidre.

Deidre walks over to Shelly and notices the scars on her back.

She grazes Shelly's scars with her blade.

Then she says sardonically, " Oh, what are these!"

Shelly jumps up and flips out the switchblade towards Deidre.

Shelly shouts, "BACK OFF, DON'T YOU TOUCH ME!"

Deidre and Shelly are at a standoff, with their blades facing one another.

Deidre says sardonically, "Ooh, looks like Barbie wants to play!"

The two sisters grab Shelly from behind; Shelly drops her blade.

Deidre says, "Fine, let's play!"

Deidre charges and then cuts Shelly's abdomen repeatedly. Shelly screams in pain

Deidre begins to toy with Shelly, gently caressing Shelly's cheek and chin.

Deidre says sardonically, "Aww, what a pretty face."

Deidre cuts Shelly's cheek and laughs.

Shelly kicks Deidre in the stomach, causing her to drop her blade as Shelly breaks free from her sisters.

She then picks up Deidre's blade and cuts all three of the sisters, the first two in the hands and stomach, before cutting Deidre's left cheek.

Shelly slashes at Deidre's arms and legs, causing Deidre to scream throughout; however, this alerts the gym teacher, who quickly grabs Shelly restraining her.

Chapter 13: Creed

Shelly, Deirdre, and Tommy find themselves in the principal's office, all three sitting across from their principal, Mister Creed.

Mr. Creed can be best described as an African American man; his hair is short and neat with a beard to match; he is dressed in a dark brown blazer with matching slacks and a white button-down shirt with a red tie.

Mister Creed starts to speak in a deep but kind voice.

"I'm surprised to see you all in my office today. Can someone please explain to me what happened?"

Deidre says, "Well, I was just getting dressed in the girl's locker room, and Shelly attacked me."

Tommy shouts, "THAT'S A LIE!"

Deidre tries to produce her best crocodile tears and begins to cry.

Tommy says, "Mr. Creed, you can't believe this! Look at Shelly's face, look at what Deidre did to her!"

Mr. Creed asks, "Tommy, I heard there was a fight regarding switchblades. Do you know how dangerous those weapons are?"

"Yes, sir." Tommy says.

Creed continues, "As you know, Miss Deidre is a very respected member of this school district; she's an honor student, top of her class, and even did some charity work if I'm led to believe."

Shelly says, "She's lying, Mr. Creed; you have to believe us! She started the fight!"

"Oh, and just where did you get the switchblade from Miss. Davis?" he asks.

Shelly sighs in frustration.

She tries to get the words out and says, "From..."

She sighs and tries again.

"From..."

"From me". Tommy says.

"Tommy, don't!" Shelly says.

Tommy stands up and says.

"I gave her that switchblade Mr. Creed, because I wanted to protect her, and I couldn't exactly go into the girl's locker room myself; I don't care about Deidre's reputation! I already know she'll get off the hook, and we'll probably get suspended, but don't suspend Shelly; she was just defending herself; suspend me instead."

Shelly smiles timidly.

Creed thinks, then says, "Hmm... I'm sorry, Tommy, I have no substantial evidence to suggest that Deidre was the one that started the fight; as far as I'm concerned, Miss Davis might have instigated it."

Tommy sighs in frustration.

Then he says, "Mister Creed!"

Mr. Creed says, " I'm sorry, I'm going to have to suspend you both and report this to your families; Deidre, you can go back to class."

Deidre says politely, " Thank you, Mr. Creed."

Tommy shouts, "What?!"

Shelly shouts, "NO!"

Deidre looks at Tommy and Shelly before saying in a sadistic and quiet tone that they could only hear.

"You kids have fun now."

Deidre heads back to class.

Shelly begins to panic, placing her hands on the side of her head, breathing frantically, tears coming down her face.

Shelly says, "Do you have any idea what they'll do to me? I don't think I could take it! Tommy."

Tommy hugs Shelly and tries to calm her down.

Tommy says, " Shh. It's okay. It's okay! You can stay with me."

Shelly is frantically sobbing, "But they'll find me, Tommy, they'll find me."

Tommy says, "Let's go, Shelly."

The two exit Mister Creed's office.

Chapter 14: Prince Charming

Shelly and Tommy are standing in the hallway just outside Mister Creed's office; Shelly has finally calmed down.

"What am I going to do?" she asks.

"Stay with me." Tommy says reassuringly.

"With you, isn't it just you and your mom? And doesn't she work all the time?" Shelly asks.

Tommy gently takes Shelly's hand.

"Yeah, but that doesn't matter; whatever you need, if I have to get a job, I will." he says.

Shelly turns away bashfully and thinks, at first unsure, but then she smiles.

Tommy puts his hand on Shelly's shoulder.

Then he asks, "Hey, umm, there's a monster movie playing at the drive-in tonight, my mom's off work. I could take her car. Would you want to see it?"

Shelly turns to Tommy, still smiling, and playfully teases him.

"Aww, Tommy, sounds like a date!"

Tommy turns bright red.

"No! Umm. I mean."

Tommy laughs nervously as he scratches the back of his head as Shelly giggles.

"I mean. I figured it would take your mind off today, at least."

Shelly replies, "First, the way you stuck up for me back there and now this? I'm starting to think you really are Prince Charming." Tommy replies jokingly, "Yeah, I guess I am."

He laughs nervously again.

Shelly grabs Tommy's jacket and gently pulls him close, causing Tommy once again to turn red.

"I'd love that; pick me up at 8, okay?" she says.

"Okay." Tommy says.

Shelly starts walking to class; she turns to Tommy.

"You coming, Tom Tom?" she asks.

Tommy immediately snaps out of a romantic daze.

"Oh yeah… right."

Chapter 15: Date Night

Later that night, Tommy and Shelly sit in the car at the local drive-in with Tommy in the front seat and Shelly in the passenger, waiting for the movie to start.

Tommy flips through the radio stations when he lands on an interesting news report.

"Suspects have yet to find a man known as the West Virginia killer, Daniel West. Police have found several dead bodies of young girls."

Tommy turns off the radio.

The two joke, "Can you believe that?" Tommy says.

"I know." Shelly replies.

They both laugh.

Tommy says sarcastically, "Ooh, the big spooky Killer's coming to get you!"

As Shelly laughs, he wiggles his fingers as he makes ghost noises.

Shelly says sarcastically, " Oh no, he's coming to get me!"

They laugh again.

A moment of silence passes.

Shelly asks, "So what's this movie called?"

Tommy says, "The Ape man, I think?"

The movie begins. Tommy pulls out a small bag of popcorn from his jacket.

Shelly asks, "Where'd you get that?"

Tommy offers the bag to Shelly.

"Does it matter?" he asks.

Shelly takes a handful and smiles.

"Nope." Shelly says as she eats the popcorn.

Tommy says jokingly, "Hey, you can hold my hand if you get scared."

Shelly says sarcastically, "Yeah, right, me scared, cute Tom Tom, real cute."

As the movie progresses, Shelly puts her hand on the seat of the car, then slowly, in a very subtle motion, grabs Tommy's hand; they both glance at each other, smirk, then continue watching the film.

Chapter 16: I Have To Go

Later, when the credits are rolling, Tommy looks over at his right shoulder and notices a sleeping Shelly resting against it. He then gently leans her up in the passenger seat and perceives to drive back to his house. He pulls into the driveway, gets out of the car, and carries her to the door. Once inside, he lays her down on the living room couch.

He retrieves a pillow and blanket from his upstairs bedroom, gently lifts her head and places it on the pillow, then slowly tucks her in with the blanket.

He begins to head upstairs to his room when Shelly wakes up. "Hey. Where are you going?" she says Tommy

replies, "I'm going to bed."

"Hey, thanks for tonight and all; sorry I fell asleep at the end." she says.

Tommy chuckles, then casually says, "It's no problem, you know that."

She sits up and stretches.

"I should probably head home" she says.

Tommy asks, "Are you sure? You could stay the night."

"There's something I have to do." she says.

Tommy asks again, "You sure you'll be all right? I don't want them hurting you again."

Shelly walks over to Tommy and gently grasps his shoulders with pleading eyes.

"I'll be okay." she says.

"Shelly." Tommy says.

Shelly touches Tommy's cheek.

Tommy leans forward as if preparing to kiss Shelly.

She regretfully turns away, then proceeds to walk home.

Shelly quietly sneaks into her home and into her bedroom, grabs the doll from the shelf, and speaks in a whisper. "Today was a great day!"

She listens to the doll.

"No, he didn't." she

listens again.

"Almost."

She regretfully looks away and sighs.

She looks back at the doll. "Yes, I know, tomorrow night."

Chapter 17: Nightfall

The next day Shelly receives her beating, as usual, by her father, only this time, even though she can feel the pain, her thoughts are on nightfall as she seems to almost tune it out, along with the words of her father saying..

"Where the hell have you been? You were out all night, girl. I bet you were out with that boy! You're not going out with no boy, not on my watch!"

Later that night, Alice is hanging clothes outside in the backyard while Alfred is asleep in his recliner. Meanwhile, Shelly grabs a butcher knife from the kitchen counter and slowly creeps up behind her father; Alice comes back inside with a basket of laundry in hand, just in time for her to see Shelly aggressively sawing into her husband's neck until his head hits the floor.

Alice stops dead in her tracks and drops the basket. Shelly, with burning hatred in her eyes, stares at her mother.

Alice motions to go left, Shelly does the same, then they both center. Alice then starts running for the back door and makes it halfway before Shelly pulls her by the hair back inside. Then Shelly mounts her mother and aggressively starts stabbing her, driving the knife deeper and deeper.

The blood splats on Shelly's face and in her hair with each stab, frequently twisting the knife into her mother's skin until Alice dies, her screams becoming a dying gasp in the pool of her own blood.

Shelly pants slowly before her breath turns into laughter. She then takes the bodies and puts them in the basement furnace, burning the evidence.

Chapter 18: Suspicion

We find the psychiatrist back in the asylum with Shelly, in disbelief but slightly fascinated by what Shelly had just recalled, jotting down his notes as usual.

As he is writing, he says, "I see. How fascinating, Tommy seems to be quite the character, a true friend, maybe more?"

Shelly smiles and blushes.

Then he asks, "And your parents, are you sure that it was you who…"

"Yes." she says.

The psychiatrist thinks, "Hmm. I see… well, we're going to have to continue this tomorrow." he says.

"Okay, thanks for listening again, Doc." she says.

"You're making great progress, Shelly; I'll see you tomorrow." he says.

The orderlies, once again, are patiently waiting for Shelly. They kindly and quietly take her doll from her, then gently take her away.

The psychiatrist curiously looks at his notes; a hint of suspicion forms in his mind as he says to himself, "Yes. But something about this doesn't add up."

Chapter 19: Aftermath

The next day the psychiatrist is waiting for Shelly, sitting in his chair, as usual, reading some old newspapers.

He notices an article; this only adds to his ongoing suspicion. "Interesting…" he says.

The orderlies bring Shelly in, as usual, then exit the room.

The psychiatrist puts the newspaper next to him on the floor, then picks up his notepad that has been sitting on his lap and starts to write.

He then asks, "Shall we continue? Tell me what happened after."

She replies, "Oh yeah, that. Well..."

Chapter 20: Hallway Part 2

A week after Shelly and Tommy's suspension, the two meet in the hallway, ready to go to the next class; Shelly greets Tommy with a smile and a hug.

Tommy smiles back and jokingly says.

"Hugs already? I haven't done anything yet."

Shelly replies in a coy manner, "You didn't have to; that was just for the little date we had."

Tommy blushes and nervously chuckles and says.

"That wasn't a date. I was just doing something nice."

Shelly replies in a coy tone, "Ok, whatever you say." "Anyway,

we should probably start heading to class." he says.

"Okay, let's go." she says.

They start walking side-by-side, when Shelly grabs Tommy's hand, Tommy notices and blushes.

"Umm... Shelly…"

Shelly audibly answers, "Hmm?"

"Your hand?" he says.

Shelly smirks at Tommy.

She says in a teasing manner, "You don't mind, do you, Tom Tom?"

Tommy blushes and says in a casual but slightly high octave.

"No... that's… fine."

Shelly then hears a group of girls giggling from across the hall.

She and Tommy turn and notice Deidre and her two sisters.

Shelly stares at Deidre with hateful, rage-filled eyes and says sternly.

"Let's go, Tommy!"

"Just pay them no mind." he says.

The two turn and head off to class, Shelly glancing back, with fiery eyes, before facing forward, quiet aggression on her face, as the gears in her mind start to turn.

Chapter 21: Payback

Later during gym class, Shelly quietly follows Deidre and her sister to the girl's locker room, armed with Tommy's switchblade.

As the girls get dressed, she hides in an alcove of one of the walls and finds a fuse box.

When she pokes her head out slightly, but still hidden from the girls, to listen to their conversation.

Deidre asks, "Did you hear that Blondie's back?"

Dee Dee replies, "Dead girl's back, huh?"

Deidre says, "Yeah, with boyfriend in tow!"

Dot says sarcastically, "Aww, how sweet, maybe they can share a coffin together for those lonely nights!"

The sisters laugh.

Shelly scowls, turns to the box, and opens it.

She says to herself, "Let's see how you girls like it when I leave you in the dark!"

She cuts the power with the switchblade; the room goes dark.

Deidre shouts, "Fucking shit!"

Dee Dee whines, "As if this place wasn't faulty enough!"

Dot asks, "Maybe they have a backup generator?"

Deidre says, "Just find the fuse box, then find someone to fix it."

A small fluorescent light flickers and buzzes back on making the room a dark blue.

Deidre says sarcastically, "Well, there's your back generator."

Dot stumbles in the dark and makes her way to the outside of the wall; Shelly gabs Dot and slices her neck. The rest of the sisters turn to hear the gurgle of Dot drowning in her own blood.

Deidre calls out, "Dot?"

Dee Dee asks, "Dottie, are you ok?"

Deidre then asks Dee Dee, "Go check on her."

Dee Dee says, "I'm scared, Deidre."

Deidre growls, "I SAID GO check on her!"

Dee Dee, still frightened, says, "Ok."

Deidre grabs her switchblade from her left stocking.

Meanwhile, Dee Dee follows a trail of blood, is grabbed by Shelly, and is aggressively stabbed to death, as she lets out a final scream.

Deidre backs up against a locker. Dee Dee's body falls from behind the wall to the floor, her eyes still open in shock.

Deidre screams, her blade now shaking in her hands.

"Who's there?!" she shouts.

Shelly steps out slowly from the wall with a bloody switchblade and a wicked smile on her face.

Shelly says in a sadistic musical tone, "Oh, Deidre."

Shelly begins to walk closer and closer as Deidre pleads for life.

Shelly corners Deidre up against the locker.

Deidre begs, "Look, Blondie, I'm sorry."

Shelly says sarcastically, "Oh, you're sorry, well…" She

slaps her hand on the locker just next to Deidre's head.

Deidre breaks out in a terrified slob.

Shelly puts her blade up to Deidre's neck, then glides the blade gently across Deidre's cheek.

Deidre begs again, "Please..."

Shelly says, "Aww, what a pretty face."

Deidre slobs louder.

Shelly smiles wickedly.

"Let's play…" she says.

Shelly grabs Deirdre by the hair, opens the locker, and begins crushing Deidre's head from the inside, using the door. Deirdre screams throughout, her body tense as it shutters with each slam. The body then goes limp; Shelly slams the door one last time, blood splatters all over Shelly and the lockers, and the squishing of flesh and the crunching of bones are heard as the body stays in place.

Chapter 22: Innocent?

Back in the present day, the psychiatrist had just taken in Shelly's story, digesting it, but it was not sitting well.

With his hand on his chin and his mind in deep thought.

Shelly, with a look of confusion and concern, as she gently strokes her doll.

"Everything ok, Doc?" she asks.

The psychiatrist says, "Hmm... yes... I'm just trying to put the pieces together, Shelly, and if my assumption is correct, you may be innocent." Shelly, now confused, says, "Innocent? I don't understand."

"We will, once we have more information, same time tomorrow Shelly?" he asks.

"Ok, Doc."

Chapter 23: More Information

The next day the orderlies bring in Shelly as usual.

The psychiatrist seemed unusually tense and extremely focused on the notepad in his hands, despite the lack of sleep shown in his bloodshot eyes.

"Well? What are you waiting for!?" he says sternly.

His statement takes her by surprise as Shelly responds with an "Oh! Um..."

He regretfully sighs, then says, "I'm... I'm sorry, Shelly, you see I've been up all night, reviewing your case… and… I haven't slept much."

"That's ok, Doc." she says.

She smiles, then says sincerely, "I'm just glad you're listening."

The psychiatrist smiles back, "Continue." he says.

She nods with a smile and says, "Ok."

Chapter 24: Phone Call

Back at the Davis household, Shelly is wrapped in a towel, drying her hair with its twin; as she steps out of the bathroom, the phone rings.

Shelly drops the towel for her hair and answers the phone.

"Hello?"

She smiles, "Hi, Tommy!" she says excitedly.

"Hi, Shelly." Tommy says.

"Hey, I just called to make sure you were alright; you hadn't been at school for a few weeks, and to be honest, I was worried." he says.

"Aww." she replies.

In a concerned tone, Tommy says, "Everything at home ok?"

"Yeah." she answers.

"Are you sure?" he asks.

"Yeah." she replies, then says, "I quit school, Tommy."

This takes Tommy by surprise as he replies, "Really? Did THEY do anything?"

"No, they went on vacation." She replies.

Tommy, now confused, says, "Vacation? Really? That's odd?"

Shelly laughs, then says jokingly, "I don't know, I think it's kind of a blessing".

"Did say where they were going?" he asks. "Don't know." she says.

He then asks, "What about, for how long?"

"Don't care." she says casually.

Tommy becomes a bit suspicious "Ok?" he says.

Then he asks, "And they just left you?"

"Yup." she says casually.

This doesn't ease Tommy's suspicion. "Right."

He then continues with… "Hey, listen, if they end up being too long, you could always stay at my house; I mean, I'd hate for you to be stuck with the bills."

"Thanks, Tom Tom, but I think I'll be fine right here." she replies.

"Ok, if you say so." he says.

Then asks, "Did you hear about Deidre and her sisters?"

"No." she says.

"They're dead, Shelly, murdered, I think; I mean, that's what everyone says at school anyway, that's why I was worried. I thought something had happened to you."

Shelly replies, "Aww, that's sweet. Do they know who it was?"

"They think it was the guy we heard on the radio." Tommy says.

Shelly says in a teasing manner, "You mean during our date?"

Tommy laughs nervously.

Tommy, now embarrassed, says, "It wasn't… it wasn't a date!"

Shelly begins twirling her hair and says, "Hmm… I don't know; you practically almost kissed me."

Tommy chuckles again nervously.

Tommy, still embarrassed, says, "Yeah…" He then clears his throat.

Then he asks, "So did you get that important thing done, the one you mentioned on our quote unquote date?"

Shelly sighs, then says unenthusiastically, "Yeah.."

"Yeah? What was it?" he asks.

Shelly replies, "Daddy needed me to dig a few holes for the night shift."

Tommy replies, "Really? That late at night? Sorry to hear that, Shelly."

Shelly says casually, "That's ok; you wanna come over tomorrow?"

Tommy asks, "Is that ok?"

Shelly says flirtatiously, "My daddy's not here to stop you, Tom Tom."

Tommy laughs, then says jokingly, "I don't think I've ever been to your house before."

"First time for everything, Tom Tom." she says, still flirtatiously.

Tommy laughs again.

Shelly asks excitedly, "See you tomorrow?"

Tommy says, "Ok, see you tomorrow."

Shelly says excitedly, "Ok, bye!"

Shelly, in giddiness, hangs up the phone.

Chapter 25: The Gifts

The next day, Tommy stands outside Shelly's home, armed with a Ramones record and a bag with a porcelain doll inside; he rings the doorbell.

The door opens, revealing Shelly, standing there with a glowing smile, dressed in a black skull and crossbones T-shirt, tied in a Daisy Duke style, ripped blue shorts, with black boots.

She greets Tommy with a warm and almost giddy hug.

"Hiya, Tom Tom, good to see ya!" she says.

Shelly excitedly takes Tommy by the hand.

"Come in inside."

She leads him into the house.

She notices the record and smiles.

"What ya got there?" she asked.

Tommy glances at the record and says, "Oh, this, just a little Ramones. I picked it up last weekend."

"Let me see." she asked; Tommy handed her the record.

Shelly looks at the cover and says, "Rocket to Russia, huh?"

Tommy says, "Oh, and this is for you." He

hands her the bag.

Shelly smiles as she pulls out the doll.

The doll is a little girl with blonde hair, blue eyes, a white dress, and matching shoes.

"Oh, Tommy, she's beautiful." she says.

She kisses and caresses the doll as Tommy smiles.

"I couldn't help but think of you when I saw her in the store window last weekend." he says.

"Aww." she replies.

She hugs him, then heads into the den, places the record and the doll down on the coffee table, unplugs the record player, picks it up, and turns to Tommy with a smile.

As she playful twirls the extension cord and winks at Tommy, all the while saying.

"Come on; my room's a better dance floor anyway."

Tommy grabs the record and follows her into her room.

Chapter 26:
Do You Wanna Dance?

Shelly places the record player on the floor and plugs it in.

Tommy sits on the bed, admiring the front and back of the album sleeve.

She turns to Tommy; she says in a coy tone, "How about a little music maestro?"

He looks up and smiles and says, "Sure."

He then hands her the record; Shelly looks at the track listing and places the needle.

The song "Do you wanna dance" starts to play.

Shelly offers her hand to Tommy, "Care to dance, Tom Tom?" she says.

Tommy blushes as he laughs nervously.

"Come on; I won't bite." She says in a coy tone.

Tommy takes Shelly's hand, and the two start dancing.

Shelly hops in place as she waves her arms to the beat and shuffles her hips and shoulders towards Tommy; he is reluctant at first but joins in as he spins her around thrice. As they're dancing, Shelly turns inward, putting her back against Tommy's chest; Shelly looks up at him and smiles as he blushes back.

She spins outward, still holding Tommy's hand in a Tango motion.

With Tommy's back facing the bed, Shelly begins teasing him with her dances, causing him to back up farther toward the bed.

They both trip and fall into bed, with Shelly falling on top of Tommy.

Shelly giggles and says flirtatiously, "Well, ain't this a predicament."

Tommy's face turned bright red, and he quickly rolled away from Shelly in embarrassment to the left side of the bed.

"Tommy." Shelly says disappointedly.

Tommy is now focused on his lap.

She scoots towards him, slowly motioning her hand while saying, "Come on, Tommy, I said I won't bite."

Tommy sighs, "We're not kids anymore, Tom Tom." she says.

Tommy replies, "I know I just..." he pauses and sniffs the air.

Shelly, now confused, says, "What's the matter?"

Tommy says, "Something... something smells... rotten."

He sniffs the air again, Shelly chuckles nervously.

Shelly then says in a nervous tone, "You know, I probably burned something in the oven. You know my cooking could kill ya, Tom Tom."

She laughs even louder as she becomes even more nervous and says… "I'm really sorry; let's just go back to dancing."

Tommy, now suspicious, says, "No..." he turns off the music and follows the smell.

Chapter 27: The Smell

Tommy makes his way to the kitchen, from a walk to picking up the pace as he heads to the basement.

Shelly is sprinting from far behind while saying.

"No, no, no! No!"

She finally reaches the opened door of the basement.

She hurries down the steps to find Tommy, stunned in horror, as he'd already found the charred bodies of her mother and father stacked on top of each other.

"Jesus..." Tommy says.

Shelly looks at the ground and begins to sob.

"I was gonna tell you eventually..." she says.

Tommy leans forward to get a closer look

"Oh god..." he says.

Shelly brushes her hair away from her face as her hands tremble.

"I just didn't want you to find out this way." she says.

Tommy places his hand over his face and sighs as he shuts out the horror he'd seen for a level head.

"Let's talk upstairs." he says.

Shelly reluctantly heads upstairs with Tommy.

Chapter 28: Confession

The two turn and face each other in the kitchen, Shelly's eyes woefully affixed to the ground.

"Tommy, I just... don't what to say..." she says.

"There's one thing I gotta know." he asked.

"What's that?" Shelly asked.

"Deidre and her sisters…" he said.

Her eyes dart up to Tommy's.

"Did you kill them?" he asks.

Shelly is silent as she looks back at the ground and nervously brushes away her hair from the right side of her face.

"Shelly..." he says sternly.

Shelly clasps Tommy's hand sincerely.

"You know what they did to us, what they did me!" she says.

Tommy's hand falls by the waist side.

"I know." he says sincerely.

Tommy takes Shelly by the hand as Shelly looks down reluctantly.

"I had to…" She said.

She begins to sob and says. "I just… couldn't take anymore."

Tommy puts his hand on Shelly's cheek.

"Shelly, you need help." he says.

Shelly turns away and asks, "What do you mean?"

"I mean professional help." he says.

Shelly turns with wide eyes as panic brooded in her voice.

"You mean, put me in some CRAZY house?!"

"No, no, not like that, doctors, Shelly, people to help you." he says calmly.

Shelly starts clutching the side of her skull with both hands, shaking her head back and forth while frantically saying. "NO, NO, NO, NO!"

She begins to pace back and forth as Tommy tries to reason.

"Shelly, LISTEN, please!"

Shelly quickly grabs a knife from the island, and slightly raises it.

Tommy cautiously backs away and puts his hands up.

Tommy says calmly, "Put the knife down, Shelly."

Shelly looks on with tear-filled eyes.

"Don't let them put me away, Tommy."

Tommy says sincerely, "They won't; the doctors will take care of you, I promise."

Tommy walks up to Shelly and says.

"Now put the knife down."

Shelly slowly lowers the knife with the help of Tommy's hand as she counties to sob.

"That a girl, come on."

"Let me just call them."

Shelly raises the knife as Tommy's eyes open wide.

"Wait!" Tommy says, and in a blind panic, Shelly stabs Tommy; as the blade pierces his flesh, Shelly stops in haste, realizing what she has done.

Shelly catches Tommy as he's dying in her arms.

"OH, GOD! NO, NO, NO, NO, NO!" She shouts.

Tommy gasps for air as blood fills his lungs, his eyes pleading with fear, as he dies with one last quiet breath.

Shelly is sobbing loudly in his chest. Then, she lifts her head to wail at the sky in a mixture of anger, pain, and sorrow.

Chapter 29: Diagnosis

"So that's why I'm here, Doc, I checked myself in after that, and here we are."

The psychiatrist sits in his chair, silent, taking in the information.

"Doc?"

He answers, "Hmm... I see..." then asks...

"Shelly, do you know what your diagnosis is?"

This phrase confused her. "Diagnosis?" she says.

"Yes, you see, you suffer from a major case of Schizophrenia." he says.

Shelly asks, "So what does that mean, Doc?"

The psychiatrist replies, "It means that you hear voices, Shelly, like your little doll friend, in which you told me, helped you plan the murder of your parents."

Shelly looks down at the doll in her hands with concern, then back at the psychiatrist.

"So, I'm crazy." she says.

The psychiatrist pauses and puts his pointer finger up to kickstart an explanation.

"Not necessarily. You see, while you confessed to those alleged murders, I researched another murder case, the case of Daniel West." "Do you remember the West Virginia killer? You briefly mentioned him."

Shelly's confusion slowly turns to realization, "Yeah, he was on the radio during..." she pauses and sighs.

"During me and Tommy's date." she says woefully.

"Correct." he says.

Shelly then asks, "What does that have to do with me, Doc?"

"Everything, Shelly, another symptom of Schizophrenia is the inability to distinguish reality from fantasy. I've done some research on Mr. West's victims, and not only do the victims match up, but the way they were killed during the same period of time."

Shelly, now confused, "So you're saying I didn't do it? But I was their Doc! I saw, heard, and..."

Shelly's eyes tear up, "felt everything."

The psychiatrist gently places his hand on Shelly's own and hand her a tissue.

Shelly wipes her tears away.

"Thank you." she says.

"Of course," the psychiatrist says.

Shelly asks, "So it's all a lie?"

The psychiatrist puts his pointer finger up again and explains.

"On the contrary, I believe you were there, Shelly, not as the culprit but as a witness."

Shelly's eyes open wide.

"As for the girls, I believe you saw a headline after the murder and fabricated the details based on what you read."

Shelly says, "That makes no sense. I killed them, Doc!"

The psychiatrist looks into Shelly's eyes.

"Think back, Shelly." he says.

"Wait." she says.

Flashes of distorted memories ripple across Shelly's mind. In her place is Daniel west, flash to the murder of her parents, while Shelly stood huddle in the corner of the room, covering her ears, trying to block out the terrifying screams all the while, in a state of tears and terror herself.

Shelly returns to the present day, now in a fit of tears.

The psychiatrist tries to calm Shelly.

"It's going to be alright, Shelly." he says.

Shelly slowly stops crying. Shelly calmly breathes in and then out as the room falls silent.

A moment passes, then she speaks.

"So…" she exhales, "Now what, Doc?" she asks.

The psychiatrist smiles and gets up from his chair.

Shelly stands up and faces him.

"I have an idea. This is unorthodox, I know, but going to arrange the courts to let you go." he says.

His statement takes her by surprise.

"But why?" she asks.

"Listen, I'm going to give you a second chance, Shelly. I am going to give you a house, a small lovely little cottage home out in the woods."

Shelly smiles as she gently places her doll on the ground next to her and happily hugs the psychiatrist.

As they embrace, tears of joy shine in Shelly's eyes.

"Thank you. Thank you so much!" she says.

She faces him and brushes her hair aside.

"You know in all this time; I never got your name?" she asks.

The psychiatrist extends his hand to shake; he says facetiously, "Doctor James Sullivan at your service!"

The two shake hands, and Shelly laughs.

"I think I like 'Doc' better." she says.

"If you say so." James says.

Shelly asks, "So when do I leave, Doc?"

"Well, if everything goes well, a month." he says.

"Oh, really! So soon!" she says excitedly.

"Yes." he says.

Shelly then giggles with excitement.

He smiles back.

Chapter 30: A New Home

A month passes, and James accompanies Shelly to her new cottage home in the woods; as the sun shines a warm yellow glow, Shelly, with the doll in hand, is wearing a blue floral-patterned dress with white sandals. The color black is gone from her nails and eyes, giving her a radiant glow.

"This is it, Shelly." James says.

Shelly gazes in amazement at the little cottage, looking like a small rural country home, white with a red door and a black roof, a small dark brown wooden porch with a white railing, and a pathway to the door surrounded by flowers of all colors.

Shelly hugs James tight as a tear-filled smile lights up her face.

Shelly says, "Thank you so much, Doc. I really don't know how to repay you."

James says, "There's no need. Shall we go inside?" In

excitement, Shelly gleefully takes James's hand.

Shelly says excitedly, "Yeah, come on, let's go!"

The inside of the house is a warm county home greeting personified, small yet cozy, with a dining room, bathroom, bedroom, and kitchen. The kitchen has white floral-pattern walls, red roses, brown hardwood floors, pristine white counters, a built sink, a green telephone, and a window to the outside with white silk curtains. Shelly placed her doll on the counter and parted the curtains to let in some sunlight; Shelly gave a relaxed sigh.

"It's beautiful, Doc." she says.

James smiles and offers his hand.

"Shall we make our way to the dining room?" he says.

Shelly takes his hand.

Shelly replies, "Sounds good to me."

The dining room is small, matching the white of the kitchen, with two wooden chairs and a circular table, with one window and a sliding door to the outside. The two sit in the dining room together as the sun begins setting, giving an orange glow as they face one another.

James asks, "Is this everything you ever wanted?"

Shelly nods and says, "Yes, again, I can't thank you enough."

"Doc, um..."

She reaches out, places her hand on his own, and gently rubs it.

"James, thank you."

James smiles, pats her hand, and moves his hand away, then replies...

"Let's keep this professional."

Shelly puts one elbow up on the table and twirls her hair.

Shelly, now slightly defeated, says, "Right... professional…"

James stands up, "Speaking of; I have to go, Shelly." he says.

Shelly quickly stands, "Go? So soon? Can't you stay a little bit longer?" she asks.

James cocks a reassuring smile.

"Here, Shelly."

James hands her a piece of paper.

Shelly looks at it to find a phone number.

"If this ever happens again, if you experience any symptoms, or if you just need someone to talk to..." he says.

James winks

"I do make house calls."

James walks out the front door. "So

long, Miss Davis, happy trails."

Shelly stands outside, waving.

"Goodbye Doc."

Chapter 31: Note

With James gone, Shelly decides to take her doll and inspect the bedroom. The bedroom has a full-size bed with white floral-patterned bedding, blue flowers, white walls, a window to the right of the room, white silk curtains, and brown hardwood floors.

But something catches Shelly's eye, a small dusty shelf just by the window.

Shelly walks over to the shelf, then blows and wipes dust away.

A note is revealed, and she reads the note aloud.

"Just a little home for your little friend, sincerely your friend James."

"Oh, how nice." she says; she begins to place the doll on the shelf when she stumbles and drops the doll.

The doll hits the floor; its face cracks open slightly.

"Oh no…" she says. She picks up the doll, its porcelain face shattered, something fleshy and oddly familiar underneath.

Shelly looks closely at the doll's face.

She is horrified to find Tommy's face skinned and placed where the doll's face should be.

"Tommy?"

She starts to breathe heavily, then looks away, then looks again.

There is nothing there but a broken shell of the doll.

Her breathing slows as she reassures herself.

"No... no…"

THE END

Milton Keynes UK
Ingram Content Group UK Ltd.
UKHW040631280723
425958UK00001B/103

9 781088 215845